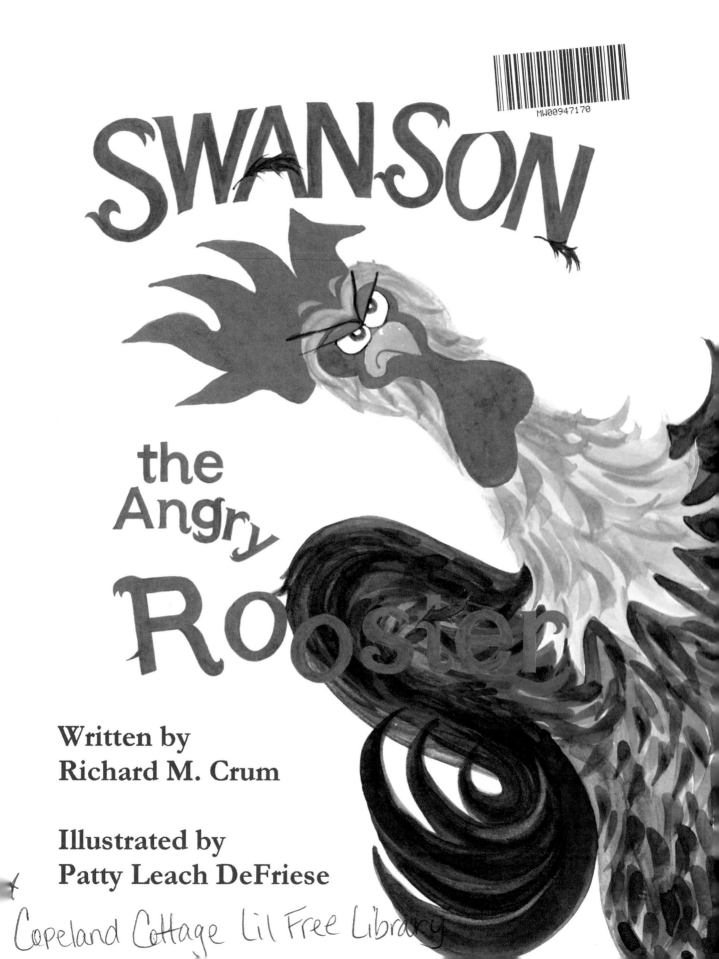

SWANSON
the Angry Rooster

Written by
Richard M. Crum

Illustrated by
Patty Leach DeFriese

Swanson is angry. He can't find anyone to be his friend. He is strutting from farm to farm trying to find a friend. But he doesn't know how to make a friend.

Swanson is so worn out and sad his feathers are droopy. If only he had a friend. Nearby is the last farm on the road. It looks so peaceful. It's his last chance to find a friend.

To make a friend, Swanson thinks he has to be rough and tough. He ruffles his feathers to make himself look bigger, opens his eyes wide to look wild, and swaggers toward Farmer Bob.

Swanson pounces on Farmer Bob
in a most unfriendly way.

8

"Let's play!" Swanson shouts,
but his sharp claws scare Charlie,
Farmer Bob's Old English sheepdog.

Mrs. Bob is coming
home from the grocery
store. Swanson glares
at her, thinking how to
make her his friend.

Swanson gives Mrs. Bob his best rip-roaring greeting. But his way of making a friend shakes up Mrs. Bob.

Church ladies paying a visit to Mrs. Bob get Swanson's hair-raising *Hello!*

Running for his life, the mailman tries to escape Swanson's scary way of saying, "Let's be friends."

Swanson tries again to make Charlie
his friend. What will he do to make
Charlie like him?

Surprise! Charlie pins Swanson to the ground. "Quit being a bully," Charlie barks. "Be KIND. Be GENTLE," he growls.

Swanson can't believe what is happening. Charlie is teaching him how to make a friend. A perky hen is watching. Swanson blinks. "Who's that?"

It's Fanny Feather Fluff! How can Swanson impress her? Strut his stuff? Or do what Charlie told him to do — be kind, be gentle. He takes a deep breath. He lifts his wing in a gentle wave. Fanny Feather Fluff answers back with a big friendly wink. Swanson is thrilled. At last he's made a friend. And what a CHICK-YODELING SPLENDIFEROUS friend she is!

26

Swanson's angry eyes turn into hearts of love.

"Fanny Feather Fluff," he crows, "I'm madly in love with you." Suddenly the farm is peaceful again.

27

Swanson's lovely Fanny
Feather Fluff shows him
how cozy love can be.

The End.

Dedications

Dedicated with love to my son, Robert Noel Crum. His real-life adventure with a rogue rooster on his acreage inspired this story. ~ Richard M. Crum

To my husband Bruce, and our grown children Jesse Blythe, Jared, and Jacob who would love to live on this farm. Thank you for letting me relentlessly bounce ideas off of you. I love you SO. ~ Patty Leach DeFriese

Swanson the Angry Rooster

Story by Richard M. Crum
Illustrations by Patty Leach DeFriese

Children's Picture Book
Rated G for all audiences

Story & Illustrations ©2021 Richard M. Crum

Color Paperback Edition
EAN 978-1-941278-99-4
ISBN 1-941278-99-X

Dragonfly Logo ©2001 Terri L. Branson
Kittycat Books Logo ©2004 Terri L. Branson
Published in the United States of America by

Dragonfly Publishing, Inc.
Website: www.dragonflypubs.com

Made in the USA
Coppell, TX
07 July 2021